The Gingerbread Donut

Give To Those Who Need

AuthorHouse™
1663 Liberty Drive
Bloomington, IN 47403
www.authorhouse.com
Phone: 1 (800) 839-8640

Published by AuthorHouse 02/25/2019

ISBN: 978-1-5462-7698-2 (sc)
ISBN: 978-1-5462-7697-5 (e)

Print information available on the last page.

Any people depicted in stock imagery provided by Getty Images are models, and such images are being used for illustrative purposes only.
Certain stock imagery © Getty Images.

This book is printed on acid-free paper.

authorHOUSE®

The Gingerbread Donut

Give To Those Who Need

Bri B.

I dedicate this to my grandmother
who is very giving.

One day Miss Malcomen decided to make donuts for her grandchildren that were coming over.

As she started to make the donut she noticed that there was something different about it. But she couldn't seem to find what was so different. As she gazed closely at the donut. The donut started to bubble and grow so big. It was bigger than any donut, and grew ginger legs and ginger arms. She tried to climb above the donut to see what was going on.

All of a sudden the donut had two legs and two arms that popped out of the donut. Miss Malcomen opened her eyes so wide and was in so much shock!

"I didn't want to make a gingerbread man, I just wanted to make a Donut", shouted Miss Malcommen.

"You made a Gingerbread Donut!" Shouted the Gingerbread donut.

The Gingerbread Donut ran outside of the house and didn't look back. He was afraid that the old lady would trap him or eat him.

Down the path the Gingerbread Donut ran. But he was stopped by a big box! The big box had all of these colors. The box was big and it looked magical. The Gingerbread Donut decided to drag the box with him.

On the path he ran into a fox that looked a little lonely.

"Hello" said the Gingerbread Donut.

"I am lonely because I don't have any friends", said Foxy.

"Why is that?" asked the Gingerbread Donut.

"I just am a grumpy fox and I don't know how to be sweet, but you are sweet because you are made out of sugar", said the fox to the Gingerbread Donut.

"I am sweet because I have my manners, not because of all the sugar I am made out of", replied the Gingerbread Donut.

The Gingerbread Donut wanted to help and looked in the magic box. Sugar magically appeared and he handed the fox a bucket of sugar.

"This should make you more sweet and kind after you start eating it. But, you must show your manners to others", said the Gingerbread Donut.

The fox licked the sugar and his paws.

"I feel sweeter already, I guess I have some manners in me somewhere it must be the sugar", said Foxy the fox.

"Thank you" said Foxy

"You have manners already", replied the Gingerbread Donut.

It started to rain and the fox ran away. The rain started to come down a little and the Gingerbread Donut became a little wet.

On his way down the path he ran into a bird named Sally.

"Why do you look so sad"? Asked the Gingerbread Donut.

"I am sad because I bumped my beak and it is so soar. Now, I can't dig for worms and have a nice meal to eat tonight on this rainy day.

"You cannot pout because you have a problem that you have to solve", said the Gingerbread Donut".

The gingerbread donut looked into his magic box and pulled out a shovel. He dug a hole in the ground and out came a worm.

"Thank you so much" said the bird.

"What did you learn"? Asked the Gingerbread Donut.

"When there is a problem you can fix it", said Sally the bird.

"You are welcome", said the Gingerbread Donut.

The Gingerbread Donut went on down the path and saw a turtle moving very slowly. The turtle started to cry as it walked slower.

"What's wrong"? Asked the Gingerbread Donut",

"I am a slow moving turtle that is stuck in the rain and no one has stopped to help me", said Tommy the turtle.

"Did you ask someone for any help"? Asked the Gingerbread Donut.

"No "replied Tommy the turtle.

"That is why, you have to use your words for people to know you need help"? Said the Gingerbread Donut

"Ok" replied Tommy the turtle.

"I need help moving faster because it is so rainy out", said Tommy the turtle.

The Gingerbread Donut smiled and opened up the magic box.

"Here is a skateboard it will get you anywhere for anytime", said the Gingerbread Donut

"Ok" said Tommy the turtle.

The turtle hopped on the board and was moving really fast.

"What did you learn"? Asked the Gingerbread Donut.

"To try not cry", said Tommy the turtle.

The turtle skateboarded away and was gone before the Gingerbread Donuts eyes.

The Gingerbread Donut went on down the path. There he saw a cat that was climbing the tree.

"What are you doing climbing that high tree"? Asked the Gingerbread Donut.

"I am trying to stay dry because the rain has wet me up so much", said Cathy the Cat.

"I don't want you on that tree and it doesn't look safe", Said the Gingerbread Donut.

"Why"? Asked the cat.

The cat slowly lost her balance and fell almost off the tree. She was hanging by one branch on the tree.

"Come down from that tree before you hurt yourself", said the Gingerbread Donut. The cat came down and looked at the Gingerbread Donut.

"I know that you do not like the rain, but you have to be safe", said the Gingerbread Donut. The Gingerbread Donut looked in its magic box and pulled out an umbrella.

"What a box!" said Cathy the cat.

"It is magic", said the Gingerbread Donut

"What did you learn"? Asked the Gingerbread Donut

"Being safe is the best way!" said Cathy the cat.

The Gingerbread Donut watched the cat walk under the umbrella.

"Stay dry and no more climbing trees in the rain", said the Gingerbread Donut.

"Thank you", replied the cat.

Down the path the Gingerbread Donut went. The rain started to pour harder, but the Gingerbread Donut didn't let that stop him.

He was stopped by a big green frog that looked so grumpy.

"Why do you look so angry"? Asked the Gingerbread Donut.

"I have not eaten all day because I can't catch flies", said Freddy the Frog.

"Now move out of my way", said Freddy the frog in a stern voice.

"Now the problem you are having can be solved, but you have to have a softer voice", said the Gingerbread Donut.

"I need to eat now!" Said Freddy the frog.

"The rain is everywhere and I can't catch any flies. Everytime I stick out my tongue I can't catch a fly to eat. I lick raindrops because of the rain", said Freddy the Frog.

The Gingerbread Donut wanted to help, so he looked in his magic box.

"Here is a basket of trash, the flies will come to it", said the Gingerbread Donut.

"OH Thank You!" said Freddy the Frog.

"I promise after I eat, I will not be a grumpy Frog", said Freddy the Frog.

"You should never be Grumpy always find a way to be happy", said Gingerbread Donut.

Down the path the Gingerbread Donut went. Where he saw a duck that looked sad.

"What's wrong"? Asked the Gingerbread Donut.

The rain has stopped people from coming to the pond. Now I can't eat any bread, and I really want some bread.

"OH please OH please! I need some bread", said the duck.

The Gingerbread Donut pulled out a buttered brown toasted bread out of his magic box and handed it to the duck.

"Oh thank you Oh thank you!" said the ducky.

"The rain will go away, it won't be forever no need to be sad ", said the Gingerbread Donut.

The Gingerbread Donut started walking down the path. He started to smile because the rain slowly came to an end. He had helped a lot of animals on the way. Yet, he still had to keep going, the day wasn't over. He looked up to the sky and saw dark clouds. The rain was going to come back soon. The gingerbread donut kept going down the path.

There he saw a bunny hopping down the path.

Hello said the Gingerbread Donut

"Hello", said the bunny.

"I have been hopping down this path and I have not had a single snack all day", said the bunny.

"Let me help you", said the Gingerbread Donut

"Here is one big carrot ", said the Gingerbread Donut as he pulled it out of his magic box.

The bunny was so happy he hopped more and more. He had a lot more energy after eating the big carrot snack.

"Thank you!" said the bunny.

"You are welcome ", said the Gingerbread Donut.

The Gingerbread Donut left the bunny and went on down the path. On the path he saw a Puppy that looked wet and sad.

"What is wrong?" asked the Gingerbread Donut.

"I got locked out my house and I can't find my bone to chew on", said the puppy named cutie.

The Gingerbread Donut felt bad and handed the puppy a bone from the magic box.

She licked the bone and was so happy.

"Thank you!" said cutie the puppy.

"Your welcome", said the Gingerbread Donut.

The Gingerbread Donut went on with his day. When he ran into a huge pig along the way.

The pig looked sad and didn't know what to do, so he sat there and began to pout.

"What happened piggy"? Asked the Gingerbread Donut.

"I have no friends' because I smell bad." said the piggy looking sad.

"You are a pig you are not supposed to smell sweet, don't you love mud!" said the Gingerbread Donut.

"It would be nice to not be so sticky" said the piggy.

"Just so I can have friends", said the piggy.

"Let me see if I can help", said the Gingerbread Donut.

The Gingerbread Donut pulled out a bar of soap and a bucket of water.

He soaped up the pig and poured the bucket of water on the piggy.

"Now your all clean", said the Gingerbread Donut.

"Thank you", said the piggy.

"Now, I can find friends because I do not smell anymore I am as sweet as you", said the piggy.

"Your welcome", said the Gingerbread Donut.

The Gingerbread Donut went on the path with his magic box, which was full of magic and had helped many others. The Gingerbread Donut was thankful for the magic box. But, before you knew it the Gingerbread Donut was stopped in the path again. The sun was starting to come out very slowly and the Gingerbread Donut began to smile.

"Hello" said the Horse

"Hello "said the Gingerbread Donut.

"Do you have any toys that I can play with in that magic box?" asked the horse.

"I am bored and I have nothing to play with. I need something to make me smile", said the horse.

The Gingerbread Donut who loved to help, pulled out a pair of sunglasses and a book for the horse to read.

"Thank you", said the horse.

The sun came out and the horse knew that it was now time to use his sunglasses.

The Gingerbread Donut walked down the path. He felt so good about himself and the sun shined on him. I am so happy that I was able to help others. I gave them goods from my magic box and I was able to teach and help them fix their problems. The Gingerbread Donut opened the magic box one last time, and out popped a Gingerbread house!

The Gingerbread Donut had somewhere to stay. Deep down inside he believed the magic box gave him the biggest gifts already, because with those gifts he was able to help others in need. The Gingerbread Donut truly believed the more you give the more you receive! The night began to fall, the Gingerbread Donut had made it to a magical home just in time.

The sun slowly faded and it started to snow, the Gingerbread Donut thanked the magic box for all it gave!

The Gingerbread Donut truly believed the more you give the more you receive! He received the biggest gift that he was truly in need.

THE END

Printed in the United States
By Bookmasters